The Flood

The Flood

Emile Zola

Translated by Anthony Cummins

Published by Hesperus Press Limited
28 Mortimer Street, London W1W 7RD
www.hesperuspress.com

'The Flood' first published as 'L'Inondation' in *Le Capitaine Burle*, 1882
'Blood' first published as 'Le Sang' in *Contes à Ninon*, 1864
'Three Wars' first published as 'Trois Guerres' in *Madame Sourdis*, 1880

First published by Hesperus Press Limited, 2013
Introduction and English language translation © Anthony Cummins, 2013
Selection © Hesperus Press, 2013

Designed and typeset by Fraser Muggeridge studio
Printed in Denmark by Nørhaven

ISBN: 978-1-84391-188-3

CONTENTS

INTRODUCTION

It rained non-stop for two weeks in the south of France during the summer of 1875. The Garonne – the 400-mile-long river that springs up in the Pyrenees, running northwest through Toulouse and Bordeaux – burst its banks, killing more than 1,000 people in the towns and villages that it swamped under nearly twelve metres of water. Days later, a newspaper reported that 'the stench arising from the ruined quarter of Saint-Cyprien at Toulouse leads to the supposition that many bodies are yet lying beneath the stones of the fallen buildings'.

Zola relished this kind of detail. At the time of the disaster, he was still trying to establish his reputation. 'Although he works from morning until night and lives extremely modestly, he can hardly make ends meet,' observed his friend Ivan Turgenev. 'He stays at home all the time with his wife, never puts his gloves on, and doesn't have a suit.' Unlike Turgenev (the son of an heiress) Zola enjoyed no private wealth. His much-needed fees from journalism had dwindled after two of the newspapers for which he wrote were shut down, and the unimagined income from *L'Assommoir* (1877) – the harrowing novel of drink and debt that gave Zola his first taste of international celebrity – remained some time away. But there was hope. While his recent book *La Conquête de Plassans* (*The Conquest of Plassans*, 1874) had flopped, with 170 copies sold in the six months since publication, its surprising popularity abroad won Zola a handy gig as the Paris correspondent of *Vestnik Evropy* (*European Herald*), a St Petersburg monthly. Among the regular, lucrative '*Parizskie Pis'ma*' ('Letters from Paris') that he contributed was 'Navodnenie' – 'The Flood' – 'a sort of short story', as Zola told his editor, featuring 'the most tragic and most affecting incidents' from 'the floods that have laid waste to our southern districts'.

'The Flood' was written within a month of the disaster and possesses, in miniature, the characteristic attributes that animate Zola's better-known fiction. It is told from the perspective of Louis Roubieu, a wealthy seventy-year-old farmer who lives in a village on the Garonne. The title is the story's own spoiler. Plot has no role to play, and even if the past-tense narration plays its usual trick – lulling you into forgetting that *it's already happened* – Louis tells us at the beginning, more or less, what we will have learned by the end. 'The Flood' relies on horror, not suspense. Zola revels, as usual, in the gruesome particulars that most of his literary contemporaries prefer to ignore: the water that remorselessly suffocates our narrator's son-in-law flows from the same pen as the boozy vomit that splatters Coupeau's bedsheets in *L'Assommoir* or the weeping sores that pockmark the ruined prostitute heroine of *Nana* (1880). As with the final pages of *L'Assommoir* – when Coupeau's widow Gervaise is discovered, 'already green' – we may feel that Zola is not observing tragedy but instead indulging an appetite for narrative rubbernecking. Yet the story's afterlife invites us to soften so harsh a judgement. When the Garonne overflowed once again, in 1930, a special edition of 'The Flood' raised relief funds for its victims, nearly three decades after Zola's death. Henry James once said that 'Zola's naturalism is ugly and dirty, but he seems to me to be *doing something*'; perhaps the remark contained more truth than James knew.

'Blood' ('Le Sang', 1863), the second story presented here, dates from an earlier phase of Zola's career, when his reputation was even less certain. In this eerie tale, which is among the first pieces that he succeeded in getting printed, four soldiers embroiled in an unspecified war find themselves haunted by bizarre, quasi-biblical visions. Zola composed it in his early twenties. He had been living in Paris for four years, working by day at a prominent publishing house, and afterwards returning – as he proudly told his childhood friend Cézanne – to his Latin Quarter digs to 'shut myself in my room and read or write until midnight'. Placing the fruit of this labour required pluck:

> I am an employee in the publicity department of the bookseller Hachette. There I've been able to read *The Review of the Month* and admire your great passion for youth and freethinking. Won't you extend some hospitality towards an unknown who has precisely nothing to recommend him save these very qualities of youth and independence?

La Revue du Mois, a newish periodical that Zola had turned to after rejections from more prestigious magazines, did not acknowledge the poems accompanying this plea. Zola took the hint and, undaunted, sent two stories instead; 'Blood' was used straight away. The sense of fulfilment may have been fleeting – as soon as Zola considered *La Revue du Mois* a reliable outlet for future work, it folded – but, nonetheless, the publication of this story was an encouraging step towards his first book, *Contes à Ninon* (*Stories for Ninon*, 1864). Like the other pieces in that collection, 'Blood' is hardly trademark Zola. Reviewing *Contes à Ninon* under the cover of anonymity – a canny act of self-promotion that *was* trademark Zola – he drew attention to the story's 'icy surrealism': this, from the author who would declare, at the peak of his literary fame, that 'the imagination' had no place in fiction, a novelist being 'nothing more than a court clerk… who simply records what he has seen'. Yet, despite its apparently unnaturalistic extravagance, the never-ending surge of gore in 'Blood' – again the story fulfils the title's promise – reminds us that Zola is rarely the sober stenographer that he pretended to be in polemical essays like *Le Roman expérimental* (*The Experimental Novel*, 1880). His novels may originate in research trips and note-taking, but often they climax with cartoonish excess: the appalling study of peasant life *La Terre* (*The Earth*, 1887), for example, has a woman preside over the rape of her pregnant younger sister, whose belly she then shunts into a sickle, before setting fire to the murder witness – their elderly father – as he sleeps.

Where Zola sometimes intended such ghoulishness to focus public attention on iniquitous government policy – *La Terre* targeted rural land law – the grotesque element in 'Blood' makes a more indiscriminate protest, 'expressing horror at violence and war', as he said in his self-penned review. Three years before he wrote 'Blood', French troops fought to rid Italy of Austrian occupation; and three years before that, they fought to preserve the Ottoman Empire in the face of escalating Russian aggression. That never-ending surge of gore had a basis in reality. But 'Three Wars', the last item in this volume, shows that Zola was no peacenik. First published in May 1877 – nearly seven years after the French Emperor Napoleon III issued a disastrous declaration of war on Prussia – it was an-other of the *Parizskie Pis'ma*, and it responded to recent events as quickly as 'The Flood' had. Zola promised *Vestnik Evropy*'s editor that he would 'try and talk to your readers about battles, our friend Turgenev having told me that all thoughts point that way, in Russia'. He was alluding to the Russian Empire's latest war on Turkey, which began in the Balkans one month before 'Three Wars' appeared. Under such circumstances pacifism would not do. Rather than 'expressing horror at violence', Zola's semi-autobiographical account – some of it expediently adapted from earlier French journalism – shows its allure, telling the story of the Crimean War (1853–6), the Second War of Italian Independence (1859) and the Franco-Prussian War (1870–1) as experienced by two school friends, the brothers Louis and Julien. Though Zola narrates, he stays intriguingly offstage. In the last instalment, when Napoleon III declares war on Prussia, there is only the merest hint – and it needs fairly strenuous interpretation – that our speaker is the busy thirty-year-old who is about to embark on the twenty-volume *Rougon-Macquart* novel cycle, with the achievement of *Thérèse Raquin* (1867) already behind him. 'Zola' just shuttles around Paris, seemingly without ambition, as his friends are drawn deeper into the conflict, the city's siege approaching. The real Zola was in Marseille; more to the point – as his self-effacement discreetly implies – he was exempt from military service, being the only son of a widow (square that with his bellicose opening paragraphs). By the time 'Three Wars' was published, Zola could self-efface as much as he liked: *L'Assommoir* had been published, and all Europe knew his name.

– *Anthony Cummins, 2013*

A Note on the Text

These translations are based on the texts of 'L'Inondation', 'Le Sang' and 'Les Trois Guerres' as collected in Henri Mitterand's edition of the *Oeuvres complètes* (Paris: Cercle du Livre précieux, 1966–70), vol. 9. 'L'Inondation' was first published in Russian ('Navodnenie', *Vestnik Evropy*, Aug. 1875) before appearing, in Zola's original French, in the collection *Le Capitaine Burle* (Paris: Charpentier, 1882). 'Le Sang' was first published in *La Revue du Mois*, Oct. 1863, then collected in *Contes à Ninon* (Paris: Hetzel & Lacroix, 1864). The book was translated into English as *Stories for Ninon* by Edward Vizetelly (London: William Heinemann, 1895). 'Les Trois Guerres' was first published in Russian ('Moi vosponninaya iz voennyx epox', *Vestnik Evropy*, Apr. 1877), then in French ('Mes souvenirs de guerre', *Le Bien Public*, 10, 17 and 24 Sep. 1877), before appearing, under its eventual title and with the introduction that is translated here, in the multi-authored collection *Bagatelles* (Paris: Dentu, 1892). Edmund Gosse translated it into English, in *The Attack on the Mill: and other sketches of war* (London: William Heinemann, 1892).

The Flood

1

My name is Louis Roubieu. I am seventy. I was born in Saint-Jory, a village several miles up the Garonne from Toulouse. For fourteen years I fought with the earth to keep bread on the table. Then the good times came; last month, I was still the richest farmer in the village.

It was as if we were blessed. We had a happy home; the sun was on our side, and I don't remember one bad harvest. There were nearly a dozen of us at the farm, living in this bliss: I was leading the young ones to work, still able to hold my own; my younger brother Pierre, who never married – he was a retired sergeant; and my sister Agathe, who moved in with us after her husband died – a formidable woman, stout, carefree, with a laugh you'd hear from the other side of the village. Then there was the whole gang: my son Jacques, his wife Rose, and their three girls Aimée, Véronique and Marie. Aimée was married to Cyprien Bouisson, a great strapping fellow who was the father of her two little boys; one aged two, the other ten months. Véronique was only just engaged; she was going to marry Gaspard Rabuteau. And Marie, she was quite the young lady – so fair, so blonde, she looked like a city girl. That was ten, counting everyone. I was a grandfather and a great-grandfather. At mealtimes, I had my sister Agathe to my right and my brother Pierre to my left; the children closed the circle, sitting oldest to youngest, their heads decreasing in size, right down to the ten-month-old who was already tucking in to his food like a grown man. All you'd hear would be the sound of spoons scraping plates! The kids could eat all right. Mealtimes were always great fun. 'Give us some bread then, granddad!' I felt a surge of pride and joy whenever the little ones reached their hands out to me. 'A big slice, granddad!'

Those were the days! We all worked hard. Then in the evenings Pierre invented games and told us stories about his regiment. On Sundays Aunt Agathe made pancakes for the girls. Marie sang hymns like a choirgirl; with her blonde hair falling around her shoulders, hands clasped to her pinafore, she looked like a saint. When Aimée married Cyprien, I added another floor to the house; laughing, I said we'd need to raise it again once Véronique and Gaspard got married. If we'd kept building an extension for every new couple, the house would have ended up in the heavens. We didn't want to move out. We'd more likely have built an entire town on our own land! When the different generations get along so well, it's nice to be able to live and die in the place where you grew up.

We had a gorgeous May this year. The crops hadn't promised so much in a long time. One day I did the rounds with my son Jacques. We were gone for nearly three hours. Our pale green meadows stretched out along the banks of the Garonne; the grass was a good three feet tall, and already there were shoots a yard long on the willow bed that we planted last year. We checked on the fields that we had bought up one by one as the money rolled in; the wheat grew plentifully, and our vines were flourishing. It would be a great vintage. Jacques laughed, poking me in the shoulder.

'Well, we'll not be wanting for bread and wine any more, eh? You must have cut a deal with the good Lord himself for him to decide to rain money on us like this!'

We often joked about the bad old days. Jacques was right. I must have made friends in high places – some saint, or, indeed, the good Lord himself – because we were having all the luck in the world. Whenever it hailed, the hail stopped just at the edge of our fields. Whenever disease struck neighbours' vineyards, it was as if some kind of wall protected our own.

After a while, I thought it was only fair. I never hurt anybody; I felt that I was owed this happiness.

On the way back, we crossed the land that we owned on the other side of the village. The plantations of mulberry trees were coming on like a dream, and the almond trees had a full yield. We chatted away, making plans. Once we had enough money, we'd buy up all the pieces of land that connected our fields, and then we would be the owners of an entire area of the village. If this year's crops lived up to their promise, our dreams were about to come true.

We were nearly home when we saw Rose calling out to us, agitated. 'Quick, hurry!'

One of our cows had just had a calf, causing something of a stir. Aunt Agathe was palpating its massive belly while the girls peered at the newborn. It seemed yet another blessing. We owned nearly a hundred animals – cows and sheep, mostly, not counting the horses – and recently we had needed to extend our stables.

'Time to celebrate!' I said. 'A bottle of fortified wine for us tonight.'

But Rose took us to one side and explained that Véronique's fiancé, Gaspard, had come to set a date for the wedding. He was staying for dinner. Gaspard was the eldest son of a farmer from Moranges. He was a big lad of twenty, renowned for his amazing strength; once, he defeated Martial, The Lion of the South, at a fair in Toulouse. For all that, he was very shy. He was an honest young man with a heart of gold; he blushed whenever Véronique looked him in the eye.

I asked Rose to call him. He was out in the courtyard helping our servants hang the washing. We were in the dining room; when he came up, Jacques turned to me. 'Say something, father.'

'So,' I asked, 'you've come to set a date for the big day?'

'Yes, Monsieur Roubieu.' His cheeks were very red.

'Don't blush, my boy. If you want, let's do it on the 10th of July. That's St Félicité's Day. It's the 23rd of June today, so you've barely two weeks to wait. Félicité was my wife's name. It will bring you happiness. So, all set eh?'

'St Félicité's Day, Monsieur Roubieu.'

Giving me and Jacques a friendly tap – he could have floored a bull – he kissed Rose, calling her Mother. He might have been a bruiser, with thumping great fists, but he was so much in love with Véronique that he couldn't eat nor drink. He admitted that he would have been ill if we had refused to let her marry him.

'Now, let's eat – you'll stay for food, won't you? I know I'm starving!'

There were eleven of us at the table that evening. We sat Gaspard down next to Véronique. He was so overwhelmed that he didn't even touch his plate, staring at her with tears in his eyes. Cyprien and Aimée smiled; they'd only been married for three years. Jacques and Rose looked more serious – they'd been together for a quarter of a century – but they still gave each other sly little looks full of love. I felt that I was living my life all over again in our two young lovers. Their happiness brought a corner of paradise to our table. We had a terrific meal that night. Aunt Agathe tried out some jokes – she always knew how to make you laugh – and Pierre, bless him, wanted us to know all about his fling with some young Lyonnaise. It was a good thing that we were having dessert, and that everyone talked over each other. I had two bottles of fortified wine fetched from the cellar; we drank to Gaspard and Véronique's future happiness. In our home a toast went like this: 'Don't fight – have lots of children – and make lots of money – good luck!' Then we sang. Gaspard knew some love songs in patois. We asked Marie to sing us a hymn. She stood up; her delicate voice tickled your ears like a tin whistle.

I had gone to stand at the window. Gaspard joined me. 'Nothing new round your way?'

'No,' he said. 'But they reckon all this rain we've been having could well mean trouble.'

It had rained for nearly sixty hours without a break. The Garonne was very full from the day before. But we trusted her. That smooth broad expanse was so bountiful that, as long as she didn't overflow, we couldn't call her a bad neighbour. What's more, if you're from the country, you don't leave your home on just any old whim – not even when the roof's about to cave in.

'Well,' I shrugged. 'It'll amount to nothing. It's the same every year. She rears up, raging, then she settles down overnight, meek as a lamb. You'll see, lad; we'll be laughing about it just like we always do. The weather's fine, see!'

It was seven o'clock; the sun was setting. The sky was so blue! It was like a velvety blue blanket, sprinkled with flecks of gold from the setting sun. I had never seen the village drift off into so sweet a sleep. The rosy tint faded from the rooftiles. I heard a neighbour laughing, then I heard some children at the nearby bend in the road; further away, there was the vague noise of distant herds trooping back to their stables. The Garonne rumbled on all the while, but I was so used to it that it sounded just like silence. The sky turned pale; the village drifted further into sleep. It was the kind of evening that you get after a fine day. All of our good fortune, I thought – our excellent crops, our happy home, Véronique's engagement – was raining down on us from the heavens. We were being blessed.

I went back to the table where the girls were busy gossiping. We were listening to them, smiling, when, in the peace and quiet of the countryside, we heard a sudden scream. It was a scream of distress – and death.

'The Garonne! The Garonne!'

2

We rushed to the yard.

Saint-Jory lies at the bottom of a hill half a kilometre from the Garonne; tall poplars on the meadows hide the river from view.

We saw nothing. Still the cry rang out:

'The Garonne! The Garonne!'

Suddenly two men and three women came running out onto the road in front of our house; one of the women had a child in her arms. They were the ones doing the screaming. They ran as fast as they could, terrified. They kept looking round nervously, as if chased by a pack of wolves.

'What's up with them?' asked Cyprien. 'See anything, granddad?'

'No. Even the leaves on the trees are perfectly still.'

It was true. There was nothing to be seen on the sleepy horizon. But I was still speaking when the others cried out; the people were running away from what looked like a pack of grey, yellow-spotted beasts, rushing over the long grass through the poplar trees. They sprang up from all sides, wave upon wave: it was a foaming, earth-shaking stampede of water.

Now we were the ones screaming.

'The Garonne! The Garonne!'

The two men and the three women were still running. They heard the terrible rushing sound get closer. The rolling waves massed together and then crashed in like troops on the charge. The first strike smashed three poplars, sweeping away leaves and swallowing up branches. It demolished a wood cabin. A wall crumbled. Unhitched carts flew away as if they were made of straw. But the water seemed to be after people most. It swirled around the steep bend in the road and flooded the plain, cutting off their escape. They kept trying to get away, splashing about, mad with fear. Now nobody screamed. The water was up to their knees. A giant wave flung itself over the woman who carried the child, and everyone disappeared.

'Come on! Come on!' I shouted. 'Get inside! The house can take it. There's nothing to worry about.'

We ran upstairs, just in case. We sent the girls up first; I insisted on being the last to go. The house was built on a mound up above the road. Though we could hear the faint sound of water creeping into the yard, we weren't very scared.

'This'll be nothing,' Jacques assured us. 'In '55, the water came in just like it's doing now; a foot of it, then it cleared up, remember?'

'Bad news for the crops, all the same,' Cyprien murmured.

'No, no, it will be nothing,' I said, seeing the girls and their big pleading eyes.

Aimée had put her two children to sleep in her bed, staying at their side together with Véronique and Marie. Aunt Agathe talked about heating the wine that she had brought up; it would give us all courage. Jacques and Rose were looking out of the window. I was at another window with Cyprien, Gaspard and my brother.

9

Our two maids were wading through the yard. I called down to them. 'Why aren't you up here? Don't stay there getting soaked.'

'But what about the animals? They're frightened. They're killing each other in there.'

'We'll see later. Come up, come on.'

Saving the livestock would be impossible if things got worse. But there was no point scaring everyone. I made an effort to sound optimistic. Leaning at the window sill I chattered on while observing the flood's progress. After the first wave of attacks, it occupied even the narrowest lanes. The water wasn't charging in any more; instead, it was going to strangle us, slowly. The dale on which Saint-Jory stood was turning into a lake. Soon the water in our yard was a metre deep. I watched it rise. But I insisted that it wasn't rising. I even said that it was receding.

'So there you are, young man.' I turned to Gaspard. 'You've no choice but to sleep here. Unless the roads clear up soon – it could well happen.'

He looked back at me, saying nothing. His face was white. I saw his eyes switch to Véronique's; the idea made him feel awkward.

It was half past eight, and it was still bright outside. The pale sky looked sad. Before they came upstairs, the servants had thought to fetch a couple of lamps. I lit them in the hope that they'd brighten up the darkening bedroom where we camped out. Aunt Agathe had wheeled out a table into the middle of the room; she wanted to get a round of cards going. She shot me a glance; she knew what she was up to – she was making sure that the children were distracted. Her cheerfulness masked great courage. She laughed in order to fight off the growing fear that she felt around her. The game started;

Aunt Agathe bundled Aimée, Véronique and Marie into chairs, stuffing cards into their hands, playing as if she wanted to win, packing, cutting and dealing, talking so much that she nearly drowned out the noise of the water. But you couldn't fool our girls. They were keeping an ear out, pale, their hands restless. Every other minute, they paused. One of them turned to me and asked quietly:

'Granddad, is it still rising?'

It was, and at a frightening rate.

'Not at all. Enjoy your game. Nothing to see here.'

Never had I been so tormented as I was then. The men all stood in front of the windows, to block out the terrifying sight. We tried to smile. The lamps cast comforting haloes of light on the table, and I remembered our winter evenings gathered around it; the room was just as cosy now, warm from our love for one another. Inside, it was peaceful; behind me, I heard the roar of a river let loose, water rising all the time.

'The water is three feet from the window,' said my brother Pierre. 'We have to say something, Louis.'

I shushed him, grabbing his arm. But we couldn't pretend any more. We heard the maddened cattle shrieking and whining in the stables. The horses were bellowing; they knew that they were about to die. You would have heard those screams no matter how far away you were.

Aimée shot up, clutching her face, shaking all over. 'My God! My God!'

We couldn't stop the girls from running to the windows. They looked out, mute and rigid, their hair standing on end. It was getting dark now. The moon cast a dull light, floating over the yellow expanse of water. The pale sky was like a shroud thrown over the ground. Smoke trailed in the distance. It was getting foggy. A day of fear was fading into a night of death.

And there wasn't a human sound to be heard; there was nothing but the roar of that sea, swollen to infinity, nothing but the bleating and braying of the animals!

'My God,' the women whispered, as if too frightened to speak. 'My God!'

A terrible crash silenced them. The animals, crazed, had burst through the stable doors. We saw them rolling along, carried in the current of the dirty water. The sheep were swept up like fallen leaves, in clumps, spinning in eddies; the cows and the horses fought to stay on their feet, then fell. Our big grey horse, especially, didn't want to die; it bucked, twisting its neck, snorting like a smithy, but the water wasn't going to let go. It snatched him up, rump first, and we watched him give in, defeated.

That was when we started crying. The tears welled up in our throats; we couldn't help it, we had to cry. We reached out to all our beloved animals, gone now; we had stayed calm, but now we wailed and bawled, mourning their death. We really were finished! The harvest was lost and the livestock had drowned. Our luck had changed in a matter of hours. God was unfair. We'd done nothing to Him, but He had taken it all away from us. I looked at the horizon and shook my fist. Our afternoon walk, the meadows, the wheatfields, the vines that we had believed were so full of promise – was all that a lie? Happiness is a con. The sun had set so softly and so peacefully on that mild evening. But it was a trick.

The water was still rising; Pierre was keeping an eye out. 'We must be careful, Louis – the water's touching the window!'

The warning lifted us from out of our gloom, and I snapped out of it.

'Money's nothing,' I shrugged. 'So long as we're all still here, there'll be no regrets. We'll be ready to get back to work.'

'You're right.' Jacques was fired up. 'And we won't be in danger. The walls are sound. Let's get to the roof.'

It was the only safe place left. The water had lapped stubbornly step by step up the stairs; it was already coming in under the door. We hurried to the attic, afraid, needing to keep close together. Cyprien was gone. I called out to him; he came back from next door, looking upset. Like him I'd noticed that our two maids weren't with us, and I wanted to wait for them. Cyprien gave me an odd look.

'Dead,' he said, very quietly. 'The corner of the shed under their room just collapsed.'

The poor things must have gone back to get their savings. He told me, still speaking quietly, that they had used a ladder as a bridge to get to the nearby building. I told him to say nothing. A shiver ran down my spine. Death had entered our home.

We joined the others upstairs, not stopping to put out the lamps. The cards were left spread out on the table. There was already a foot of water in the room.

3

Fortunately, the roof was big, and it sloped only gently. We got up through the skylight, where there was a kind of platform. We all sheltered here. The women sat themselves down. The men searched for a good vantage point. Leaning against the skylight, I scanned the horizon.

'Help must be on the way,' I said, putting a brave face on things. 'They have boats in Saintin. They'll be passing through here... Look! Down there, isn't that a lantern on the water?'

But nobody answered. Pierre had lit his pipe, almost without noticing, and was smoking so hard that he had to spit out bits of the stem after each puff. Jacques and Cyprien looked miserably into the distance, while Gaspard carried on prowling around the roof with his fists clenched, as if looking for a way out. The women were huddled in a heap at our feet, shivering in silence, hiding their faces so as not to see. Rose looked up, though. 'Where are the servants? Why haven't they come up?'

I avoided the question. She looked straight at me. 'So where are they?'

I looked away. I couldn't lie. I had felt death's chill already; now I felt it pass through our wives and darling daughters. They knew. Marie stood up and sighed before breaking down in tears. Aimée hid her two children in her skirts as if to protect them. Véronique had her head in her hands and wasn't moving any more. Aunt Agathe had turned white and was crossing herself wildly, stammering Our Fathers and Hail Marys.

For all that, the sky around us was spectacularly beautiful. It was a clear summer's night. There was no moon, but the sky was dotted with stars. It was such a pure blue that it seemed to cast blue light everywhere. It could still have been dusk, the horizon was that clear. The vast sheet of water spread out before us, glowing white as though luminous, every ripple sparkling under the phosphorescent night sky. You couldn't see any land now; it seemed as if the entire plain had been invaded. For a moment I forgot that there was any danger. I had once seen the sea like this at Marseille, and I had been transfixed by its beauty.

'The water's rising. It's rising,' said Pierre, his pipe still in his mouth. It had gone out.

The water was no more than a metre from the roof. It wasn't a sleepy lake any more. Now there were currents. The hill no longer offered protection. In less than an hour, the water had become violent and dirty, rushing at the house, carrying paving stones, clumps of weeds, pieces of wood, smashing up barrels. We heard the distant echo of water attacking walls. Poplars were cut down with a deadly crack, and houses crumbled as if they were cartfuls of gravel being emptied at the roadside.

'We can't stay here,' Jacques said, over and over. The tears of our women broke his heart. 'We must try something. Father, please, let's try something.'

'Yes,' I stammered, 'yes, let's try something.'

And we didn't know what. Gaspard offered to swim across with Véronique on his back. Pierre talked of a raft. It was crazy. At last, Cyprien said, 'If only we could reach the church.'

The church, with its little square steeple, was still standing firm above the water. There were seven houses between us and it. Our farm, the first in the village, backed on to a taller building, which in turn leaned against another property. We might be able to reach the parsonage by climbing over the rooftops. From there it would be easy to get into the church. Lots of people must have taken shelter inside already; we heard voices, though there was nobody around us. They could only have been coming from the steeple. But it was so risky getting there!

'No way,' said Pierre. 'The Raimbeaus' house is too tall. One ladder wouldn't be enough.'

'I'll go and take a look anyway,' said Cyprien. 'If it's no good, I'll come back. But otherwise we'll all go. We'll carry the girls.'

I let him go. He was right. It looked impossible, but we had to try. He had managed to get onto the next house, by lodging an iron hook into a chimney, when his wife Aimée looked up and saw that he wasn't with us.

'Where is he? I don't want him to leave me. We live together, and we'll die together.'

15

When she saw him on the roof, she ran over, still holding her children.

'Cyprien, wait. I'm coming. I want to die with you.' She insisted. He leaned over to plead with her, assuring her that he'd return, that it was for everyone's benefit. She looked wild, shaking her head. 'I'll go with you,' she repeated. 'I'll go with you. Why not? I'll go with you.'

He had to take the children. Then he helped her up. We watched them on top of the house. They trod carefully. The children were crying; she had taken them back in her arms. At each step Cyprien turned around to help.

'Get her somewhere safe,' I shouted, 'and come back quickly!'

I saw him wave, but the roaring water drowned out his reply. Soon we lost sight of them. They had dropped down to the next house, lower than the first. After five minutes we saw them again on the third roof. It must have been steep; they were crawling on their hands and knees. Suddenly I was afraid. I put my hands to my mouth and called out as loud as I could, 'Come back! Come back!'

Then we were all shouting, Pierre, Jacques, Gaspard, shouting for them to come back. They stopped for a moment when they heard us, but then they carried on. They reached the corner in front of the Raimbeaus' house. The roof was at least three metres higher than any of the others around it. They hesitated. Then, nimbly as a cat, Cyprien climbed right to the top of the chimney stack. Aimée stayed down below on the roof tiles; he must have persuaded her to wait. We saw her clearly, as if magnified, black against the clear sky, pressing her children to her breast. The horror began.

The Raimbeaus' place had been built as a factory. It was flimsy. The front of the house faced the current head on. I thought I saw it shake under the onrushing water; as I watched Cyprien walk across the roof, I had a lump in my throat. We heard a sudden rumble. The moon rose in the sky like a lamp, round and yellow, lighting up the vast lake: we were going to see every last detail of this tragedy. The Raimbeau house collapsed. When Cyprien disappeared we screamed in terror. The house sank. We saw nothing but a whirlwind of waves tearing through the wrecked roof. Then there was peace, and the surface of the water was smooth once again. A carcass of broken beams poked out from the black hole that had engulfed the house. Among the tangled debris I thought I saw something move; something living was making a superhuman effort to get free.

'He's alive!' I cried. 'Praise be! He's alive… There's a God all right!'

We laughed nervously, clapping with joy.

'He's climbing free,' said Pierre.

'Yes, yes, see,' Gaspard explained, 'watch him get a hold of the beam to his left.'

But we stopped laughing. We didn't say another word, choked with fear. We had just realised how much trouble Cyprien was in. When the house fell, his feet had got jammed in between two beams. Now he couldn't free himself. His head hung just centimetres above the water. It was sickening. Aimée was still on the next roof with her two children. Trembling, she watched her husband die. She didn't look away. She just kept on howling like a mad dog.

'We can't leave him to die this way,' said Jacques. His eyes were wild. 'We must get down there.'

'Let's shin down the beams,' said Pierre. 'We'll free him.'

As they set off for the nearby rooftops, the second house collapsed. Their route was blocked. We froze. Instinctively, we gripped each other's hands, squeezing them until we were sore, unable to stop watching this unfolding horror.

At first Cyprien had tried to keep his body straight. With incredible strength, he had kept himself out of the water and stayed horizontal. But the strain was too much. He struggled. He tried to grab a beam, throwing his hands around in search of something to cling on to. Then he gave up and fell back limp, hanging. Death took its time. The water, rising patiently, licked Cyprien's hair. He must have felt the cold around his skull. One wave splashed his forehead; the next shut his eyes. We watched Cyprien's head slowly disappear.

At our feet the women held their heads in their hands. We too dropped to our knees, arms outstretched, crying for mercy. Over on the other roof, Aimée was still standing with her children at her breast, howling into the night sky.

4

I don't know for how long we stayed in a daze. The water was higher by the time I came back to my senses. It was up to the tiles now; the roof was nothing more than a than a narrow island in a vast sheet of water. Houses must have collapsed on both sides. The sea spread out as far as you could see.

'We're moving,' Rose murmured, gripping on to the roof tiles.

She was right; we all felt like we were swaying, as if the roof were now a raft. The strong currents seemed to be carrying us along. Then when we saw the church steeple standing still in front of us, our dizziness ended; we were exactly where we'd been before, amid the rolling waves.

The water started to attack. The current had been following the road, but now it was blocked by rubble and it
was forced to surge back on itself. There was method to its
violence. Whenever a beam or some other passing hunk
of wreckage came in reach of the the current, the water
snatched it up and rammed it into the house. And now there
was no relief; the water would scoop up the tossed beam
and hurl it back to hammer the walls even harder this time.
Soon a dozen beams attacked us from all sides. The water
bellowed, spraying our feet with foam. The house groaned
under the weight of water. Already there were cracks in the
walls. We were getting battered. We thought that we were
done for; the walls would give way and throw us out into
the river.

Gaspard had ventured to the very edge of the roof. With his
mighty wrestler's arms he had managed to get hold of a beam.

'We have to fight back,' he cried.

Jacques, doing his bit, seized on a long pole that was
flowing past in the current. Pierre helped him. I cursed the
fact that age had made me as weak as a child. But our defence
was prepared. It would be three men versus one river.
Gaspard gripped his beam, ready to use it to block whatever driftwood got hurled at us. He managed to fend off the
attacks, just, tottering each time he absorbed the impact.
Beside him, Jacques and Pierre jabbed their long pole into the
water to sweep away the debris. This pointless struggle lasted
nearly an hour. Eventually the men lost their heads. They
stamped and swore and cursed the water. Gaspard stabbed it
as if he was fighting a duel, piercing its surface as though it
was his opponent's heart. The water couldn't care less. It was
calm, unhurt. It was imposssible to hurt. Jacques and Pierre
gave up, exhausted; Gaspard, running in for one last swipe,

lost his beam to the current, which grabbed it from him in order to batter us mercilessly. There was no point fighting.

Marie and Véronique had thrown themselves into each other's arms. They were hoarse, crying over and over the same frightened words that are still ringing in my ears today. 'I don't want to die! I don't want to die!'

Rose put her arms around them. She tried to reassure them. Then she looked up, trembling and, despite herself, screamed out. 'I don't want to die!'

Only Agathe said nothing. She wasn't praying or crossing herself any more. Looking around in a daze, she tried to keep smiling whenever her glance met mine.

The water was battering the tiles now. There was no hope of rescue. We still heard voices coming from the church. Two lanterns passed in the distance. Then silence reigned once more. The people at Saintin, who had boats, must have been hit first.

Gaspard was still prowling around when he called out suddenly.

'There! Come on, help me. Hold tight!'

He had a pole and he was watching an enormous hunk of black rubble drift slowly towards the house. It was a roof. It was made from solid planks that the water had torn from a shed. It was wide; and it floated, like a raft. When it came within his reach, Gaspard caught it with his pole; when he felt himself being dragged away, he called for help. We grabbed his waist and held tight. As soon as the raft entered the current, it smashed against the roof of our house so violently that we thought it would be broken to bits.

Gaspard jumped onto the raft with no hesitation. We had a chance. Pierre and Jacques held it at the roof's edge while he examined it to make sure that it was sturdy enough.

'Saved, granddad!' He laughed. 'Don't cry any more, ladies! A real boat – look! my feet are dry. And it'll carry all of us, easy. We'll be safe as houses on that!'

All the same, he thought that it wouldn't hurt to make it more solid. He caught some floating beams and bound them to the raft with a piece of rope that Pierre had pocketed when he came up from the basement, just in case. Gaspard even fell in the water at one point; we screamed, but he just laughed. He was comfortable in the water; he once swam three miles of the Garonne. He got up and shook himself dry.

'Don't waste time. Get on!' The women got to their knees. Gaspard had to carry Véronique and Marie into the middle of the raft. He sat them down. Rose and Aunt Agathe slid along the tiles and sat near the young girls. I looked over to the church; Aimée was still there. She was leaning against a chimney, keeping her children in the air, at arm's length – the water was up to her waist.

'It's okay, granddad,' said Gaspard. 'We'll pick her up on the way, I promise.'

Pierre and Jacques were already on board, so I jumped on. It was leaning over a bit on one side, but it was up to the job of carrying us. Gaspard was the last to come down from the roof. He told us to take the poles that he'd got ready, and he pointed out which ones would make good oars. He used a very long one with great skill. We let him take charge. On his word, we pushed our poles against the roof in order to get going. The boat seemed to be stuck. No matter how hard we tried, it wouldn't budge. The current forced us back towards the house every time. It was risky to keep on trying; our raft didn't look like it could survive these awful smashes.

Yet again we felt helpless. We had thought that we were saved. But the water still had us at its mercy. I was sorry that the women weren't back up on the roof; I worried that, any minute, the ferocious current would drag them away. I said that we should try to get back to our spot on the roof. 'No! Let's take another shot! Better that than die here!'

Gaspard wasn't laughing now. We tried again, pushing hard on the poles with whatever strength we had left. Then Pierre had an idea. He could go back up on the roof and use a rope to pull us out of the current. Once he jumped back down to the raft, it only needed a few strokes before we were out on the open sea. But Gaspard remembered his promise to rescue poor Aimée, who was still crying helplessly. We had to cross the street and tackle the strong current that we had just escaped. Gaspard glanced at me. I was torn. Never in my life had I made such a difficult choice. We would be risking eight lives. But – even if I did waver for a split second – I wasn't strong enough to shut out her whimpering.

'Do it. We can't leave without her.'

Gaspard's head dropped. Without saying a word, he took up his pole and got leverage wherever he could, from any wall that was still standing. We drifted past a neighbouring building, and then we passed our own stables. But when we came out into the street, we screamed. The current had us in its grip once more. We lost our balance, twirling like a leaf in the wind. Our screams were cut off by the noise of the raft smashing into our roof. There was a tearing sound as the unattached beams split apart, tossing us into the water. I don't know what happened. I remember that, as I fell, I saw Aunt Agathe splayed out, floating on her skirts. She sank without a struggle, looking up into the sky.

Pain opened my eyes. Pierre was dragging me by my hair along the roof. I slumped down in a daze and looked around. He had dived back in. I saw Gaspard and not my brother.

I was confused. The young man was carrying Véronique. He lay her down next to me and dived in again, pulling out Marie. Her face was like wax, so still and white that I thought she was dead. Then he dived in again. He searched in vain this time. He talked to Gaspard; I couldn't hear what they were planning. They came back up onto the roof, worn out.

'What about Aunt Agathe?' I asked. 'And Jacques? Rose?'

They shook their heads. Tears streamed down their faces. Jacques cracked his head open on a beam, they said. Rose wouldn't let him go, and she was swept away, clinging to his corpse. Aunt Agathe was never seen again; the current must have carried her body into the house through an open window.

I got up and looked over at Aimée on the rooftop. The water was rising all the time; she wasn't crying now. I just saw her upstretched arms holding her children above the water. Then they were all swallowed up, the water engulfing them under the sleepy light of the moon.

5

There were only five of us left on the roof. Only a narrow strip along the ridge was still dry. A chimney had just been dragged off. Véronique and Marie had fainted; we needed to lift them so that the waves didn't soak their legs. Eventually they came to. But we felt worse seeing them wet and shivering, and crying about how they didn't want to die. We reassured them in the way that you would reassure a child. Of course they weren't going to die; Death would have us to deal with first. But they didn't believe us any more, they knew damn well they were about to die. And each time they said 'die', the word tolled like a bell. Their teeth chattered as they clutched each other in despair.

We were done for. There was nothing left of the village; only a few crumbling walls. Yet the church stood firm, its steeple untouched. We could hear voices from inside. It sounded like the murmur of people taking shelter. Water roared in the distance. We didn't even hear the houses falling down like cartloads of gravel being emptied. It was as if we were ship-wrecked in an ocean, a thousand miles from land.

Then we thought we could hear the sound of oars – a gentle swooshing coming from somewhere over to our left, the rhythm becoming more and more distinct. Hope! We perked up, strain-ing our eyes to see. And we saw nothing. The yellow swathe stretched out in front of us, dotted with dark shapes. But these shapes weren't moving. They were the tops of trees, the remains of crushed walls poking up through the water. Weeds, drift-wood, empty barrels – these all gave us false hope. We waved our handkerchiefs, until, seeing our mistake, we remained none the wiser as to the source of this constant noise.

'I see it!' Gaspard shouted. 'Look! Down there, a big boat!'

He pointed at some distant speck. I saw nothing, and neither did Pierre. But he insisted it was a boat. We heard the sound of oars more clearly than ever. At last we saw something too. The shape moved slowly. It seemed to be circling us, without getting any closer. It was as if we had gone mad. We waved our arms around in fury, and we screamed until our throats burned. Then we cursed it – were they cowards or what? The black shape glided away noiselessly. Was it really a boat? To this day I don't know. It disappeared, and so did our last hope.

From then on we were just waiting to be swept away. The house was weak. It was probably being supported by nothing more than a single wall; when that went, everything would go with it. What scared me most of all was feeling the roof wobble under our feet. Maybe the house itself would have held out all night, but the roof was caving in, battered and pierced by beams. We had retreated over to the left side, where the rafters still held firm. But these seemed to be weakening too. There was no way they could take the weight of all five of us crowding into so narrow a space.

Pierre twirled his moustache, his pipe at his lips. He muttered something, and frowned. All his courage counted for nothing next to the growing threat. He couldn't bear it. He spat into the water with a sneer. We started to sink further. He made his choice, and climbed down from the roof.

'Pierre!' I was scared of having understood his intention. 'Pierre!'

He turned back. 'Goodbye, Louis,' he said softly. 'All this waiting around – it's too much. And you'll be able to spread out a bit.'

He chucked his pipe into the water, then jumped.

'I've had it. Goodnight!'

We didn't see him after that. He wasn't a strong swimmer. He'd given up in any case. His heart was broken. He didn't see the point of carrying on when our loved ones were dead.

The church bells struck two. This awful night of tears and suffering would soon be over. There was less and less dry ground under our feet. The murmur of water grew louder as the waves lapped back and forth over the tiles. The current had shifted again. A procession of debris drifted slowly to our right, as if the water was getting tired. Soon it wouldn't be able to rise any higher.

Gaspard kicked off his shoes and threw down his jacket. He cracked his knuckles.

'Grandfather. This waiting's killing me; I can't stay here with you. Let me go. I'll save her.'

He meant Véronique. How could he be strong enough to carry her all the way to the church? I said no.

'I can! I've got the muscle. I'm up to it. You'll see!'

And he wanted to go now. Hearing the house crumble under us made him feel as weak as a child.

'I love her,' he kept saying. 'I'll save her.'

I said nothing, holding Marie close. He thought I was accusing him of being selfish, of thinking only about the woman he was going to marry.

'I'll come back for Marie, I swear. I'll find a boat. I'll get help.' He was stammering. 'Trust me, grandfather.'

Stripped to the waist, he told Véronique what to do: she mustn't argue, she mustn't struggle and, above all, she mustn't be frightened. She didn't seem to understand; yes, yes, she repeated, yes. Gaspard crossed himself – he never was a regular at church – and then he slid down the roof, holding Véronique by means of a rope looped under her arms. She screamed, splashing around with her arms and legs, and then she fainted.

'That's better!' Gaspard shouted. 'Now I can do all the talking!'

You can imagine how afraid I was, watching them. The water was white; I could see everything Gaspard did. Winding the rope around his own neck, he slung Véronique over his right shoulder. At times he buckled under her crushing weight, yet he ploughed on, swimming with superhuman strength. I had no doubts now; he was already a third of the way there. But then he banged straight into a wall that was hidden under the water. It was a horrible thump. They both disappeared. Then I saw him, alone; the rope must have snapped. He dived down twice. He emerged at last, Véronique on his back. But without the rope she weighed him down more than ever. He was making progress all the same. I shuddered as they got nearer to the church. Suddenly – I wanted to scream – I saw beams, crashing down on their blindside. I watched open-mouthed. The water swallowed them up.

I was in a daze from then on. I was nothing more than an animal, finding shelter out of pure instinct. The water advanced; I retreated. I heard someone laugh over and over, not knowing who. It was dawn. It was very fresh and very peaceful. It was like being at the edge of a pond, when the water comes alive before sunrise. But I could still hear laughing. I turned to see Marie, standing in her wet clothes. She was the one laughing.

The poor sweet thing! How lovely she looked under the rising sun! I saw her crouch down to scoop some water into her palms and wash her face. She plaited her beautiful blonde hair. She seemed to think that she was in her bedroom, getting dressed to go to mass, the church bells ringing out merrily. She was still laughing, bright-eyed, her face full of joy. Her madness was infectious; I started to laugh too. Fear had turned her insane. It was a blessing – she was so happy to see this beautiful springlike morning.

I didn't understand what she was doing, so I let her go about her business, shaking my head tenderly. She was making herself beautiful for all eternity. When she felt that she was ready, she sang a hymn. Her voice was as delicate as cut glass. But she broke off, as if to answer someone who was calling her, someone who only she could hear.

'I'm coming! I'm coming!'

She started to sing again, climbing down the roof and slipping into the water. It covered her gently, without a ripple.

I was still smiling, looking on contentedly at the spot where she had just disappeared.

I remember nothing after that. I was alone on the roof. The water had risen further. There was still a chimney standing; I must have clung to it with all the strength I had left, like an animal that doesn't want to die. Then – nothing, nothing, just a black hole. Nothingness.

6

Why am I still here? They told me that people from Saintin came in boats around six, and that they found me lying on a chimney, passed out. The flood was cruel. It took away everyone I loved; why not take me too? I wouldn't have felt a thing.

I survived. All the others are gone – the children in their swaddling clothes, the girls who would have got married, the young couples, the old couples. And then me: a stubborn weed rooted right down between the stones, shrivelled and stringy – but alive! I'd do what Pierre did if I had the guts. 'I've had enough. Goodnight!' Chuck myself into the Garonne and join the others. I have no children left. My house is destroyed, and my land is ruined. How happy I was, when we sat down to eat, the old ones in the middle, the children eldest to youngest! How happy I was reaping the harvest, all of us at work together, picking the grapes, coming home proud of our riches! Our beautiful children and our beautiful vines, our beautiful girls and our beautiful crops: all my joy, the living reward for a life's work! With all that gone, God, why keep me alive?

There's no consolation. I won't take accept. I'll give my fields to the neighbours whose children aren't dead. They'll have the energy to clear up the mess and replant the crops. When you don't have children, all you need is somewhere to die.

There was only one thing I wanted. A final wish. I wanted to find their bodies and bury them in our plot, under the slab where I'd soon be joining them. I heard that many of the bodies had been carried downstream; they had been lifted out at Toulouse. I decided to go.

It was horrific. Nearly two thousand houses had collapsed. Seven hundred people were dead. Every bridge had been smashed up; a whole district lay buried in mud, razed to the ground. Twenty thousand people were dying of hunger, walking around in rags, half naked. The city stank of dead bodies; everyone was terrified of catching typhoid. There was a funeral procession in every street. Charity couldn't heal these wounds. Walking through the devastation, I saw nothing. I had my own dead to think of; I was devastated too.

They had retrieved many of the bodies, they said. A lot of them were already buried in some trenches in a corner of the cemetery. The thing is, they'd taken care to take photos of anybody that couldn't be identified. I found Gaspard and Véronique in these upsetting pictures. They had died in the middle of their wedding kiss. They were clutching each other so fiercely – mouth clamped to mouth, their arms wound tightly around their backs – that you would have had to break their bones to separate them. They were photographed together, and together they sleep under the earth.

This is all I have: this frightening photograph of two beautiful children, disfigured and bloated by the water, their livid faces fearless with their love for one another. I look at them, and weep.

Blood

After the victory, four soldiers set up camp in a deserted corner of the battlefield. Night had fallen. Corpses lay all around, and the men were having a hearty supper.

Sitting on the grass, they grilled lamb, not waiting for the slices to be cooked through before tucking in. The glowing red flames threw a flickering light over the soldiers, casting misshapen shadows far into the distance. At times the firelight glinted off the weapons strewn around them; and one might have noticed, in the darkness, some of the men who slept with their eyes open.

The soldiers laughed riotously, unaware of these eyes watching them. It had been a day of fierce fighting. Not knowing what the next day would bring, they made merry with their rations and were grateful for the respite.

Night and Death swooped down onto the battlefield; their beating wings cut through the ghostly silence.

When the food was finished, Gneuss sang. The cheerful air boomed out into the sad, gloomy night and echoed back like a dirge. The soldier raised his voice, surprised to hear this peculiar lament. An awful scream rang out from the darkness.

Gneuss stopped dead. 'Could be that we didn't finish the job,' he said to Elberg. 'Investigate.'

Elberg took a piece of burning wood from the fire. For a few moments his comrades could track his movements by the light of the flame. They saw him crouch down and prod some of the corpses. He ferreted around in the bushes with his sword. Then they lost sight of him.

Nobody spoke for a while.

'Clérian,' said Gneuss at length, 'the wolves are out tonight. Go and check on our boy.'

It was Clérian's turn to vanish into the dark.

Fed up of waiting, Gneuss and Flem huddled into their coats and bedded down around the guttering flame. They had just drifted off, when another awful scream rang out. Flem got up without a saying a word and headed for that same spot where his two comrades had vanished.

So Gneuss was on his own. The shrieks coming from that black hole frightened him. He tossed some twigs onto the fire, hoping that more light would set his mind at ease. Flames the colour of blood shot up. They cast a glowing ring on the grass. Inside it, the bushes pranced around, and the corpses seemed to twitch.

Now Gneuss was afraid of the light. He scattered the burning twigs and stamped out the flames. But when darkness shrouded him once more, he shuddered. He didn't want to hear that deathbed scream again. He sat down, and then he got up, calling out for his men. His booming voice scared him; he worried that he might be waking the dead.

The moon rose. Gneuss watched in horror as a ray of light slithered over the battlefield. The night would hide the atrocities no longer. Under this moonlight shroud the ravaged lowlands stretched out for miles, scattered with corpses and wreckage. This light wasn't like daylight; it showed you what lurked in the shadows, but only made you more afraid.

Gneuss was on his feet, sweating. He wished he could run up a hill and snuff out that pallid night-light. Now that they could see him, he wondered what was keeping the dead from rising up and taking their revenge. It frightened Gneuss to see them so motionless; he shut his eyes and waited for something awful to happen.

He was standing just like this when he felt something tepid and wet at his feet. He bent down to examine the ground and saw a thin trickle of blood. It nipped from pebble to pebble, carefree, emerging out of the darkness and into the moonlight, then winding back into the shadows like some enormous black-scaled snake with endless, wriggling coils. Gneuss jumped back, but he couldn't shut his eyes; an excruciating spasm forced them wide open, fastening them on this gory rivulet.

He watched it slowly widen and swell. The rivulet turned into a stream – a gentle, placid stream that any child could have skipped over. The stream turned into a crashing torrent, spraying reddish foam around its banks; the torrent turned into an immense, monumental river.

This river was full of bodies; they were being carried along on the glut of blood that spurted from their wounds. It was a horrible, bizarre spectacle.

Gneuss recoiled in front of the bulging river. He couldn't see over to the other side; it seemed to him that the plain was now a lake.

All of a sudden he was knocked down onto a rocky knoll. He regained his balance, before feeling a wave lap against his knees. The drifting corpses were jeering at him; their wounds turned into mouths that mocked his cowardice. The deep sea kept rising; it stained his hips. He made a huge effort to climb out, digging his hands and feet into the gaps between rocks. The rocks crumbled; he fell. It was up to his shoulders.

A pale and miserable moon was watching over this sea that reflected no rays. The light hung in the sky. The howling black sea looked like a vast portal to a cavernous void.

The waves rose, spraying Gneuss's lips with their red spume.

The noise of Elberg returning woke Gneuss at dawn. 'Mate, I got lost in those woods. I must have nodded off after I sat down for a minute under a tree. I had some really bizarre dreams; my memory's still clear even now I've been awake.

'It was back at the beginning of time. The sky was like a great big smile. The unsown soil was spotless under the spring sunshine. The grass grew taller than the tallest of our oaks; the trees were covered with leaves like we've never seen. Sap ran freely through the earth's veins, and there was so much of it that it didn't stay only in the plants; it poured into the rocks too, bringing them to life.

'A calm horizon shimmered. It was Nature, waking up. Like a child giving thanks to God for the morning light, it offered up all its scents and all its songs, lingering fragrances and inimitable music, so much so that I could hardly bear it, so holy did it seem.

'The lush sweet soil bore fruit without labour. The trees grew with abandon; the roads were lined with wheatfields, just like today's are lined with nettles. The air smelled fresh; there was no trace of our sweat. God alone worked to provide for his children.

'Man lived off the fat of the land. He picked the fruits from the trees, drank spring water, and at night slept under the shelter of leaves. Meat disgusted him. He didn't know what blood tasted like, and his palate valued only those foods that water and sunlight had made for him.

'So man stayed blameless. His innocence crowned him king of all other creatures. Everything was in harmony. You can't imagine how pure it all looked, or how peaceful it was. When the birds flapped their wings, it wasn't because they were fleeing; the forests hid no fugitives in their trees. All of God's creatures lived together under the sun as one, following one law: be good.

'As I was walking among all of this, I felt that I was becoming fitter, stronger. I breathed deep lungfuls of the air; leaving our polluted atmosphere for this cleaner world, I felt like a miner climbing back to ground level.

'I was still dreaming. This is what I saw as I slept in the forest.'

'Two men followed a narrow path through the under-growth. The younger man walked ahead; he was humming without a care in the world, enjoying the scenery. Now and then he turned back to smile at his companion. I'm not sure quite what it was, but something about his kind smile made me think the two men were brothers.

'The other one was stern. He didn't smile. He stared at the back of the younger man's neck, full of hate. He quickened his step, stumbling. He seemed to be chasing a victim who wasn't escaping.

'I saw him stop to cut down the trunk of a tree, which he hacked crudely into the shape of a club. He ran, hiding the weapon behind his back. The young man had sat down to wait for him. Hearing him approach, he got up and kissed him on the forehead, as if they had been apart a long time.

'They walked on. The sun was setting. The boy hurried, spotting a hillside's gentle slope through the trees at the edge of the forest, yellow in the dying light. The unsmiling man thought he was running away. So he raised the tree trunk.

'His younger brother turned around to spur him on for the final leg of the trek. The tree trunk smashed his skull, spraying blood everywhere.

'The grass flinched from the first drop, horrified. The earth drank it down, trembling, afraid; it screamed out in disgust, and the sandy path returned that sickening brew to the blood-stained moss.

'When the boy screamed, I saw a wind of fear scatter all the animals. They fled from the sight of people, avoiding the normal routes; they waited at crossroads, and the strongest set upon the weakest. I saw them skulk off to polish their fangs and sharpen their claws. It was the rape of the earth beginning.

'I watched a never-ending exodus. The kestrel attacked the swallow; the swallow plucked the fly from the air; the fly settled on the corpse. All creatures felt under threat, from the worm down to the lion. The world was eating itself; and it would carry on devouring itself, forever.

'Nature convulsed with horror. The horizon's clean straight line snapped. Bloodstained clouds hid the stars and sunsets. It never stopped raining. And, each year, the trees toss rotting leaves from their gnarled branches, down onto the earth.'

3

Clérian appeared as Elberg finished. He sat down between his two comrades.

'What I'm about to tell you, I don't know whether I saw it or dreamed it, so much did the dream seem real and what was real seem a dream.

'I was on a road that crossed the world. It was lined with cities, thronged with travellers.

'I saw that it was paved with black stones. I slipped before realising that they were black with blood. The road sloped on both sides; in the middle ran a stream of thick red water.

'I followed this road; there was a bustling crowd. I went from group to group, watching life go by.

'Fathers sacrificed their daughters, having promised their blood to some evil god. The girls bowed their blonde heads under the knife, turning white at the kiss of death.

'Proud shivering virgins killed themselves, fleeing kisses that would shame them; instead of white dresses, they had gravestones.

'Lovers were dying mid-kiss. One woman died on the water's edge, mourning her loss, transfixed by the waves that had swept away her beloved; another woman was murdered in her lover's arms; she flung herself around his neck, both of them dying in an everlasting clinch.

'Men who were tired of living in darkness and poverty set their souls free in search of the liberty denied to them on this earth.

'Kings trailed bloody footprints all over the road. One had walked in the blood of his brother; another, in the blood of his subjects; another, in the blood of his God. Their red footprints in the dust sent a message to the crowd: "A king was here."

'Priests butchered their victims; then, bent dumbly over throbbing innards, they pretended to unravel heavenly secrets. They hid swords in their vestments and preached war in God's name. On hearing their sermons, the people set on each other, laying waste for the glory of our father in heaven.

'All of humanity was drunk; it banged into walls, sprawling out over the flagstones soiled with hideous muck. It shut its eyes, gripped a double-edged blade with both hands, then went out for a night of slaughter.

'Shrouded in a damp thick reddish mist, the crowd breathed carnage. It roared and surged in a furious orgy, trampling down anyone who fell and squeezing the last drops of blood from their wounds, swearing with breathless rage at the corpses that no longer screamed out in pain.

'The earth swilled it all down; its guts relished these bitter juices now. Like a ruined drunk it gorged itself on the dregs.

'I pushed on; I wanted to get away from these scenes. There seemed no end to this black road; I was following its bloody flow out to some unknown sea.

'The landscape became more harsh and bleak the further I walked. The plains were tearing themselves apart. Rocky masses carved the earth into barren hills and gloomy valleys. The hills grew taller, the valleys widened; stones turned into mountains, and furrows became gorges.

'There were no leaves and no moss. The sun bleached the summits of the desolate hills; at the bottom, they were dark and shadowy. The road ran between these rocks, deathly silent.

'Eventually, after a sharp bend, I found this grim place.'

'Four mountains pushed against each other to form a vast basin. Their smooth, steep slopes rose – like the walls of some Cyclopean city – and, inside, there was a gigantic well, as broad as the horizon.

'The stream ran into this well; it was full of blood. Inside, the calm, deep sea rose gently. It seemed to be sleeping on its rocky bed. The clouds were purple with the reflection.

'It was then that I knew it was full of all the blood from all the fighting. Each wound, ever since the first murder, has wept into this gorge, so much so that it's full.'

'I saw a river running into that pit, last night,' said Gneuss.

Clérian carried on. 'I was horrified. I stood at the verge, trying to see how deep it ran. From its dull sound it seemed that it went down to the earth's core. Then I saw that the flood had reached the mountain peaks. A voice cried out to me from the void. "The sea is rising. And it will keep rising. Soon it will reach the summit. Then it will rise some more. It will burst, and flow out into the plains. The mountains will not be able to fight the flood. They will crumble. The lake will surge out over the earth. There will be a flood. And so it is that men who are yet to be born will die, drowned in the blood spilled by their fathers.'"

'That day is coming,' said Gneuss. 'The waves were high, last night.'

4

The sun was rising as Clérian finished telling the others about his dream. A bugle called somewhere to the north, the sound wafting on the early-morning breeze. It was the signal: disbanded troops were to assemble around the flag.

The three men got up, taking their weapons. They were about to set off, looking for one last time at the remains of the fire, when Flem came running through the long grass. His boots were white with dust.

'I've run so fast I can't tell you where I've been. Trees were whizzing around me. The sound of my footsteps lulled me into a weird sleep; my eyes shut but I kept on running, not even slowing down.

'I reached a deserted hill. The hot sun beat down on the rocks; I couldn't stop running because my soles would burn. I hurried to the top.

'There I was, busting a gut, when I noticed another man, climbing slowly. He wore a crown of thorns. He carried a heavy load on his shoulders, and his face was soaked in sweat. He found it hard going, stumbling at every step.

'The ground was burning hot; I couldn't watch him struggle. I climbed to the top and waited for him under a tree. Then I saw that it was a cross he was carrying. To go by his crown, and his purple robes, splashed with mud, I thought that he might be a king. So I was mighty glad to see him suffer.

'He had soldiers behind him, hustling him with pikes. When they got to the peak they stripped him and and stretched him out onto the ominous-looking cross.

'The man smiled sadly. He opened his hands nice and wide for the executioners; they banged a couple of nails in, the blood dripping. Then he crossed his feet; one nail was enough to do the job.

'On his back he looked up silently into the sky. Two tears ran slowly down his cheeks. He did not feel them, smiling as though he'd given up.

'They raised the cross. The weight of his own body stretched his wounds. It was horrible. I heard his bones crack. There was a long shudder; then, he looked back up to the skies.

'I stared at him. He was brave, in death. "This man is no king," I said. Then I felt pity; I shouted at the soldiers, finish it, stab him through the heart.

'A warbler was singing on the cross. Its song was sad; to me it sounded like a virgin's sobbing.

'"Flames get their colour from blood," it said, "flowers get their colour from blood, blood makes naked lovers blush. When I stood on the sand, my feet bled; when I brushed the branches of an oak tree, my wings bled."

'"I met a righteous man, and I followed him. I had just washed myself in the spring, and my coat was clean. I sang, Rejoice, my feathers; the rain that falls from all the killing will not sully you now, not when you're on this man's shoulders."

'"Today I sing: Weep, warbler of Golgotha, weep! Blood from the man who gave you shelter stains your feathers. He came to restore our purity, and alas! men leave him with no choice but to smear me in the dew of his own wounds."

'"My faith wavers; I weep for my spoiled coat. O Jesus! Where will I find another like you to give me shelter? O hapless lord, who will I find to wash my feathers, stained with your blood?"'

'The crucified man listened. His eyes grew heavy-lidded; death was in the air. His mouth twisted with pain. He looked at the bird in gentle reproach. His smile was as bright and peaceful as hope itself.

'Then he screamed. His head hung down on his chest, and the warbler flew away, sobbing. The skies darkened, and the earth trembled under the shadows.

'I was still running, in my sleep. It was dawn. The valleys awakened, bright under the morning mist. The sky was clear after the overnight storm; the leaves were greener for all the rain. But my path was still lined with the same thorns that had grazed me the day before; my boots crunched over the same jagged stones; the same menacing snakes slithered through the bushes as I ran. The blood of the righteous man had washed through the earth's veins, but it hadn't given back its lost innocence.

'The warbler flew overhead.

'"O, I am so sad. There is no spring pure enough for me to bathe in. See how the earth is just as wicked as it was? Jesus is dead. But the grass isn't growing… O, it's just another murder."'

5

The bugle could still be heard.

'Fellers,' said Gneuss, 'it's a dirty job. We can't sleep. We kill men and they come back to haunt us. Like you, I've had nightmares a long time. A demon squats on my chest. Here's the thing. I've been killing thirty years now; I need to get some sleep. Let's leave it to someone else. I know a place where they need some extra pairs of hands for the ploughing. Do you want to do an honest day's work for your money?'

'We do.'

The soldiers dug a big hole at the foot of a rock. They buried their weapons. They went for a wash in the river. Then they disappeared, arm in arm, around the bend in the road.

Three Wars

War! Terrible word. To Frenchmen of my generation – the generation whose fiftieth is behind them – it evokes three memories above all: the expedition to the Crimea, the Italian campaign, and the catastrophe of 1870.[1] What victories, what defeats – and what a lesson!

Granted, war is vile. It is sickening to see nations at one another's throats. Progressive liberals say that there must be no war, envisaging a time when nations will engage one another cordially. There are some thinkers, much admired, who see the world not in terms of nations, but in terms of *humanity*, and who forecast an era of universal concord. But these ideas don't last five minutes when there's a threat to the homeland! Even the philosophers grab their guns and start shooting; these declarations of brotherhood are drowned out by the cries of *kill!* that rise up from every patriotic heart. Because we have to have wars; they're a necessary evil, like death. For civilisation to flourish, you might say, you need to make sure that the dungheap is well stocked. Life is nothing without death, and wars are like those antediluvian cataclysms that made it possible for humans to live on this earth.

We have become soft; we cry over every lost life. But do we even know how many people this planet needs? *Life is sacred*, we let ourselves think. The ancient Greeks beheld terrible massacres, but they didn't then rush off and advocate some utopian fraternalism. Maybe these stoics had the more honourable view. Be a man, and accept that death goes about its strange work unseen, in the night; accept that people just die, and it so happens that they sometimes die in greater numbers. This is the rational way to think, when all's said and done, because if you get worked up about war, you have to get angry about every other human failing. Even the bellyaching, bleeding-heart intellectuals must see that war will remain the tool of progress, until we perfect civilisation and celebrate eternal peace. We are far from perfecting civilisation, and so we'll surely be fighting for centuries to come. It's the fashion, these days, to call war a hangover from our barbarian beginnings, and to say that, under the Republic, we'll be rid of it. But when that siren rings out on the border, and you hear the bugle in the street, we'll all be reaching for a gun. Because war is in the blood.

Victor Hugo once wrote that only kings wanted war – all their subjects wanted to do was to kiss and cuddle. That's nothing but a poet's dream, alas. Hugo has been the high priest of the sort of fantasy that I'm talking about. He celebrated a United States of Europe; he urged the importance of international community, and prophesied a new Golden Age. What could be nicer? But you can be brothers all you like, what matters most of all is that you love each other. And nations do not love each other. Why pretend otherwise? It's true, I admit, that a vulnerable monarch might take a gamble and declare war against a neighbour, hoping for a victory to tighten his grip on the throne. The thing is, right from the very first battle – win or lose – that war belongs to the people, and they fight for themselves; if they aren't fighting for themselves, they don't fight. And that's to say nothing about wars that really do involve the entire nation. Let's imagine, for instance, that one day France and Germany find themselves squaring up to each other again. Everyone will be fired up – and not for the sake of *the Republic* or *the empire* or *the monarchy* or *the government*. From coast to coast men will answer the bugle's call, trembling with anticipation. Whether we knew it or not, the seeds were sown twenty years ago; and if ever the time should come, war will break out over our land like an overflowing harvest.

I say it again: three times in my life I have heard the eerie sound of War beating its wings over France. It begins with a distant rustling; you think gales are on the way. The sound gets louder. There's a crash, and every heart beats faster; people turn giddy with enthusiasm as the country feels the need to conquer and kill. Then, when the men are gone and the noise has died down, an anxious silence takes over. Everyone listens out for the first cry from the army: will it be a cry of victory, or a cry of defeat? It's a terrible time. There are contradictory reports. You seize upon the tiniest scraps, analysing every word, until the hour of truth. And what an hour that is – sweet joy, or bitter despair!

1

At the time of the Crimean War, I was fourteen. I was still a boarder at school in Aix, shut away with two or three hundred other kids in an old Benedictine convent. The long corridors and vast halls retained something of its former gloominess. Its two courtyards were more cheerful, under the glorious southern skies that stretched out vast and blue. I did suffer there, but I remember that school fondly.

At fourteen, I wasn't exactly a child. But looking back today I see how ignorant we were. World news didn't reach that forgotten corner. The sad old town was a dead capital, slumbering in barren countryside, and the school, close to the fortifications, slept even more deeply. In all the time that I was cloistered there, I don't recall ever hearing anything about one single political scandal. Only the Crimean War had any impact – and it was probably several weeks before we heard about that.

I smile, thinking back to what war meant to us provincial schoolboys. It was all very vague at first. The fighting was happening in a land so distant, so strange, and so savage, that we imagined the scene to be like something from the Arabian Nights, come to life. We couldn't have told you where exactly it was taking place, and I don't think that any of us thought for a minute to look into the atlases we each had at our fingertips. Our teachers, it must be said, kept us in total ignorance of the modern world. They read the papers, they knew what was going on; but they never spoke to us about it, and if we had asked, they would have sent us packing, back to our essays and exercises. We knew nothing for certain, except that France was fighting in the Orient; why, we didn't know.

But some things we did know. We repeated the old jokes about the Cossacks; we knew the names of two or three Russian generals, and we imagined these generals to have heads pretty much like monsters, gobbling up small children. We never once thought France could lose; to us that seemed perverse. Then there were gaps. As the campaign dragged on, we forgot that there was a war on, for months at a time, until the day that some snippet of news brought us back, breathless with excitement. I can't tell you if we knew about the battles as they took place, or if we experienced the thrill of capturing Sebastopol.[2] It was all a muddle. To us, the reality was Virgil and Homer – more worrying to us than any modern-day quarrel among nations.

I do remember the game that was all the rage for a while in the playground. We split up into two groups, and marked two lines in the dust. Then we fought. It was a simpler version of prisoner's base; you had to drag the other lot over behind your line. One group were the Russians; the other, the French. The Russians were meant to lose, but sometimes that didn't happen; there was an awful, furious racket. At the end of the week, the head had to ban this charming pastime: two pupils had been brought into the infirmary with cracked skulls.

One of the most distinguished combatants was a tall fair-haired boy who always got picked to be General. Louis was from an old Breton family that had moved down south, and he looked like a winner. He was very fit and very strong. I can see him now, a handkerchief tied round his forehead like a soldier's plume, sides cinched in by a leather belt, leading his troops on, arm aloft as if he were brandishing a sword. We admired him, respected him even. Funny, he had a twin brother, Julien, who was much shorter than him, delicate and frail, and who found these games very distressing. Whenever we split into two sides, he slunk away to watch from a stone bench, looking sad and a bit frightened. One day Louis stumbled under the blows that rained down from a gang of boys, and Julien cried out, pale, shivering, swooning like a woman. The two brothers adored each other, and none of us would have dared tease the little one for being a coward; we were afraid of what the bigger one could do.

My memories of these twins are bound up with my memories of the time. Towards the spring I became a day-pupil; I didn't board anymore and came to school only for the seven o'clock classes. The two brothers were also day-pupils. We were inseparable. We lived in the same street, so we waited for each other to walk to school. Louis was old for his years, and wanted adventure; he led us astray. It was decided that we would leave for school at six, in order to have a whole hour of freedom in which we could be *men*. Being men, for us, meant smoking cigars and drinking alcohol in a seedy backstreet bar that Louis had discovered. Cigars and drink made us sick as dogs; but what a feeling when we opened the door to the bar, making sure nobody saw us, looking left, then right, before going in!

These fun and games took place towards the end of winter. Some mornings, I remember, the rain lashed down. We waded through, turning up to class soaked. When the mornings became clear and mild, we got the mad notion of going off to watch the soldiers. The road to Marseille passes through Aix; the regiments came into town from Avignon, slept a night, and then the next day made their way to the coast. At the time, more troops were being sent to the Crimea, cavalry and artillery especially. Not a week went by without troops passing through town. A local newspaper even advertised their visits in advance, to give some notice to the families where the men lodged. Only, we didn't read the paper; so our great difficulty was finding out before going to sleep whether or not the soldiers would be setting off in the morning. They left at five, so we had to get up very early. Often it was pointless.

What a happy time! Louis and Julien shouted me down from the street, where there was not a soul to be seen. I rushed out. Though the days were as mild as in spring, it would be chilly as we walked together through the deserted town. If a regiment was about to leave, the soldiers would assemble on the Cours Mirabeau, in front of the hotel where the colonel usually stayed. We craned our necks excitedly as soon as we turned the corner at the Rue d'Italie. If there was nobody there: disaster! And there was often nobody there. We missed our beds – though we'd never say so – wandering around at a loose end until seven, having no idea what to do with our freedom. What a treat, on the other hand, to turn the corner and see the Cours packed with men and horses! The cold morning was filled with a spectacular crash and clatter. The soldiers arrived from every direction, drums pounding and bugles blazing. The officers had trouble getting everyone into line. Gradually, order established itself, the ranks assembling, and we chatted to troops, darting between the horses' legs at the risk of getting crushed. We weren't the only ones enjoying the show. Shopkeepers appeared one by one; there were people with business in town; all the early risers. Soon there was a crowd. The sun rose. The gold and steel of the uniforms glistened in the morning light.

On the Cours of that peaceful town, still deep in slumber, we saw dragoons, cavalrymen, lancers, and all the branches of the big cavalry and the light cavalry. But our favourites, the ones that we were craziest about, were the cuirassiers. They dazzled us, sitting astride their stout horses, the sunlight glinting from their breastplates. Their helmets glowed under the rising sun; their ranks were like rows of suns that cast dancing rays on the houses round about. If we discovered that there would be cuirassiers leaving, we got up at four, desperate to set eyes on the performance.

At last the colonel would appear. The colours were kept safe overnight at the place where he stayed; now they were unfurled. All at once, after two or three orders were bellowed out, the troops set off. They marched down the Cours; a rising drumbeat set our hearts racing, as the first hooves clapped onto the hard ground. We ran to keep pace with the head of the column, where the band was banging out a quickstep. First, three shrill bugle notes readied the musicians; then the brass started up, drowning out everything else. The last notes died away outside the town gates, in the countryside. We turned left onto the Marseille road, a pleasant stretch lined with hundred-year-old elms. The horses trotted off, scattering a little on the dusty open highway. We felt like we were going to war too. The town was far away behind us, and we'd forgotten all about school; we ran and ran, carried away with our adventure. We went off to war once a week.

Ah, those sweet mornings! It was six o'clock, and the sun, already high, lit the land with huge slanting rays. There was a mild warmth in the chilly morning breeze. Birds flew up from hedges. The distant meadows were bathed in a pink mist. Amid this smiling horizon marched these beautiful soldiers, their breastplates glowing, the cuirassiers shining like stars. The road curved suddenly down into a wide valley. The people who had come from town followed no further; soon, we were the only ones in pursuit. We went down the slope and, at the very bottom, came to a bridge that crossed the river. Only there did we start to worry. It must be nearly seven o'clock; if we didn't want to miss school, then we had just about enough time to get there – running. Often we forgot altogether; we pressed on, playing truant, then getting up to no good until noon, hiding in the grass-covered hollows beside the waterfall. Sometimes we went no further than the bridge, sitting on the stone parapet and keeping the regiment in view as it proceeded up the opposite slope of the valley. It was a rousing sight. The road went straight up the hillside for nearly two kilometres. The horses eased up, and we saw the men get smaller, swaying rhythmically. At first each breastplate and each helmet looked like a sun. Then these suns dwindled, and soon it looked as if an army of stars was on the march. Finally, the last man disappeared and the road was empty, leaving only memories of the beautiful regiment that had passed.

We were just kids. But these sights made us serious none-theless. We watched in silence as the regiment climbed the hill, in despair at the thought of losing it. When it disappeared, we had a lump in our throat; for an instant, we kept watching the faraway rock behind which it had just vanished. Would the regiment ever return? Would it come back down the hill one day? These questions filled us with a vague sadness. Goodbye, beautiful regiment!

Our excursions tired out Julien. He wouldn't have come with us so far, but he didn't want to be separated from his brother. All the walking made him achy, and he had a phobia of horses. I remember one day that we were lying in the fields, late for school after having followed an artillery unit. Louis was giddy with excitement. We ate an omelette in town for lunch, then he took us to the river, where he was set on swimming. As soon as he was old enough, he said, he'd enlist.

'No!' Julien flung his arms around Louis's neck, white as a sheet. 'No!'

Louis laughed and called him silly.

'They'll kill you,' said Julien. 'I know they will.'

He poured his heart out to us that day, wound up by our teasing. The soldiers were very ugly. He did not see why we were so interested in them. Everything was their fault: if there were no soldiers, there would be no fighting. He hated war. It terrified him. He'd find a way to stop his brother having anything to do with it. His disgust was overwhelming. It was pathological.

Weeks and months passed. We'd had enough of the troops and had come up with another game: going fishing in the morning, then eating our catch in a run-down tavern. The water was icy; Julien caught pneumonia, and almost died. At school, we didn't talk about war. Homer and Virgil engrossed us more than ever. Suddenly we heard that France were the victors, which seemed to us only proper. Then the regiments started coming through once more, this time from the other direction. We weren't interested. Yet we did see two or three; with half the men missing, they seemed less beautiful now.

Such was the Crimean War, in France, for children cooped up in a provincial boarding school.

2

In 1859 I was in Paris, completing my studies at the Lycée Saint-Louis. As things turned out my two schoolfriends from Aix, Louis and Julien, were there too. Louis was working towards the entrance exam for the École Polytechnique; Julien had decided to plump for law. Each of us lived out.

We were no longer ignoramuses. Paris had made us streetwise. When war broke out in Italy, we were up to speed with the political goings-on that had brought things to a head. We debated the events as though we were statesmen and tacticians. At school, *the campaign* was all the rage. Boys charted our troops' progress on maps. In class time we marked the latest positions with pins; we fought and lost battles. To stay in the know, we devoured an enormous supply of newspapers. It was down to us students who lived out to bring them in. We turned up armoured from head to toe with news, our pockets stuffed and our coats bulked out with bundles of papers. They were passed around during class. We paid no attention to the lessons, instead feasting on the latest news, screened by a classmate's back. We hid the pages by cutting them into four, opening them inside our textbooks. Sometimes the teachers knew exactly what was going on. But they left us to it, with the tolerance of men who had decided to let the idle get what's coming to them.

When the war began, Julien shrugged. He was going through a phase of worshipping the poets of 1830. He never went any-where without a Musset or a Hugo in his pocket; he'd be reading them in the lecture hall.[3] If you passed him a news-paper, he'd send it on its way, disdainfully, without even so much as a glance, and then get back to his poem. To him it seemed grotesque to get excited about men fighting. But that changed, after a catastrophe that turned his whole life upside down. Louis failed his exam and, one fine day, he enlisted, just like that. He had been mulling it over a long time. One of his uncles was a general; surely, he reckoned, he'd be able to get on without having his qualifications. Anyway, he could try Saint-Cyr again, when the war was over.[4] Julien was dumb-struck when he heard. He was no longer the kid who got angry about war, protesting like a girl, but his hatred never wavered. He managed not to cry in front of us; he wanted to show that he was a tough guy. As soon as his brother set off, though, he became one of our most avid newspaper-readers. We walked together to and from the Lycée, talking about nothing else but potential battles. Each day, I remember, he'd bring me to the Jardin du Luxembourg. He would put his books down on a bench and trace a map of northern Italy in the sand. That way he could be with his brother. Deep down, he was frantic, always thinking that Louis would be killed.

Even now I can't work out why war frightened Julien so much. He was no coward. He just disliked anything physical, setting it far below the life of the mind. To live like a scholar or a poet, in a shuttered study, seemed to him our true goal on this earth. The mayhem out on the streets, the fistfights and the duelling – the stuff that puts muscle on you – seemed to him evidence of savagery. At the circus, the strongmen and acrobats and lion-tamers all deserved contempt. And he was in no way patriotic, let me tell you this now. We used to give him a lot of stick, finding it shameful; I can still see him smile, shrugging his shoulders.

One of my most vivid memories of that time is the fine summer's day when news of the victory at Magenta spread through Paris.[5] It was June – a gorgeous June, unlike what we usually get in France. It was a Sunday. We had planned the day before, Julien and I, to go for a walk on the Champs-Elysées. He was very anxious about his brother – he had sent no letters – and I wanted to distract him. I called for him at one o'clock, and we sauntered down to the Seine, with the lazy scuff of pupils who no longer have the warden watching over them. You don't really know Paris if you haven't been there on of these incredibly hot summer days. Houses cast sharp black shadows on the white pavement. Between the shuttered façades you saw nothing but a solid stripe of blue sky. When Paris is hot, I don't know anywhere that's hotter. It's a furnace; stifling, suffocating. Some corners of the city are deserted, like the quays, which layabouts abandon for the cooler groves on the outskirts. Yet how pleasant it is to stroll along the wide, quiet quays with their rows of little leafy trees, overlooking the great flowing river, buoyant with its bobbing throng of boats!

So, we were at the Seine, walking quayside, shaded by trees. Faint sounds could be heard from the river, its water rippling in the sun with sweeping silvery glimmers. There was something in the air that Sunday. Paris was getting ready to hear the big news that everyone – every *thing* even – seemed to be waiting for. The Italian campaign, which ended so quickly as we all know, had begun successfully; but so far there had been no decisive battle, and Paris had spent two days waiting for just such an encounter. The great city listened, rapt, for the faraway sound of shelling.

This memory has stayed with me very clearly: I had just told Julien how odd I felt, saying that Paris seemed spooky, when we reached the Quai Voltaire and saw, in the distance, a tiny group of people standing outside the office where they printed *Le Moniteur*.[6] There were seven or eight people, reading a poster. From the other side of the street we could see them talking animatedly, laughing. We crossed eagerly. The poster was a handwritten telegram; it said, in four lines, that Magenta was taken. The wax fixing it to the wall was still wet. That Sunday, we were clearly the first to know, in all of Paris. People came running, so desperate to find out! Complete strangers shook hands, chatting away. A gentleman with a ribbon in his buttonhole explained to a workman how the battle must have unfolded. Women laughed enticingly, and looked as if they were tempted to throw themselves at anyone who passed. The huddle grew. Passers-by were beckoned over; coachmen pulled up and climbed down from their seats. By the time we left, more than a thousand people were there.

It was a great day. In a few minutes the news had crossed the entire city. We thought we'd be the ones telling everybody, but it overtook us; we couldn't turn a corner or walk down the road without seeing happy faces. The news floated in the sunshine; it was carried on the breeze. In half an hour, the atmosphere had changed; tense anticipation had given way to jubilant outpouring. For two hours we ambled among the Champs-Elysées crowds laughing with joy. Women had a glint in their eye. *Magenta* was on everyone's lips.

However, Julien was shattered, looking as pale as ever.

'They're laughing now,' he muttered. 'Maybe tomorrow they'll be crying.'

I sympathised with his private torment. He was thinking about his brother. I joked around to try and put him at ease; Louis was sure to come home a captain, I said.

Julien shook his head. 'If he comes back at all!'

Paris lit up as night fell. Lanterns hung in every window. In the poorest homes, they had lighted candles; I even saw some rooms with just a lamp on a table, pushed against the window. It was a warm night, and all Paris came out into the streets. People sat on doorsteps as if ready for a parade. Crowds gathered at junctions; the bars and cafés were rammed. There was a smell of gunpowder in the air; kids were setting off fireworks.

I'll say it again, I've never seen Paris more beautiful. All the great things came together that day: the sunshine, a Sunday, and a victory. There wasn't the same sense of euphoria after the news came out about the crucial battle at Solferino,[7] even though that brought an end to the fighting; the homecoming was a stately affair, not spontaneous like these popular celebrations.

We got two days off out of Magenta. We got even more excited about the fighting, and were among those who thought peace had come too quickly. The school year was coming to an end. Holidays were on the way. Restless, we looked forward to our freedom; Italy, the army, and our victories all evaporated in the upheaval that followed the end-of-year prizegiving. That year, I remember, I was supposed to go down south for the summer. I was about to set off – it was early in August – when Julien begged me to stay until the 14th, the day of the homecoming parade. He was ecstatic: Louis was coming back a sergeant, and he wanted me to witness his brother's moment of glory. I said I'd stay.

The soldiers camped just outside Paris for several days; lavish arrangements were made to welcome them back. The parade would come in through the Place de la Bastille, follow the Boulevards, go down the Rue de la Paix and cross the Place Vendôme. The boulevards were lined with flags. On the Place Vendôme, large platforms were erected for Government ministers and their guests. The weather was splendid. Applause erupted along the length of the Boulevards at the first glimpse of the troops. The crowds packed in on both sides of the road. Heads piled up at windows. Women waved handkerchiefs, tearing flowers from their dresses to throw down to the soldiers. Throughout all of this the regiments kept marching past at a steady pace, to wild cries of *bravo*. The bands played; tricolours fluttered in the sunshine. Many of them were riddled with bulletholes; the crowd applauded, showing special appreciation for one flag that was shredded and draped with spoils. An old woman standing at the corner of the Rue du Temple dived into the marching ranks to hug a corporal; her son, I suppose. The good lady was almost carried away on the tide of joy. There were soldiers in tears.

Place Vendôme was the venue for the official ceremony. Ladies in their frocks, magistrates in their gowns and civil servants in uniform all clapped respectfully. There were speeches and presentations. In the evening, the Emperor hosted a banquet of three hundred at the Louvre, in the Salle des États. He made his celebrated speech over dessert: 'If France has done so much for a friendly people, what would she not do for her own independence?' Unwise words, which he must have regretted later.

Julien and I had watched the parade from a window on the Boulevard Poissonnière. The day before, he had visited the army camp and told Louis where we'd be. As his regiment came by, Louis gave us a nod. He had aged tremendously, his face bony and weathered. At first I didn't recognise him. Compared to us – we were pale and delicate, like women – he looked like a man. Julien watched him for as long as he could keep him in sight, and I heard him murmur, with tears in his eyes, shaking with emotion:

'Beautiful… It *is* beautiful…'

That evening I met them in a café in the Latin Quarter. It was a quiet tiny place down a backstreet, where we often met to talk undisturbed. By the time I arrived, Julien was already engrossed in Louis's tales of Solferino, listening with both elbows on the table. Never was a battle more unexpected, Louis said. The Austrians were supposed to be pulling out. The Allied troops were on the march when suddenly – it was around five o'clock on the morning of the 24th – they heard gunfire. The Austrians had done a U-turn and outflanked us. Skirmishes broke out involving each division in turn. The generals fought all day long – but, isolated from one another, they had no clear idea of the overall pattern that the battle was taking. Louis had taken part in fierce hand-to-hand combat, in a cemetery, in the middle of all the graves; that was about as much as he'd seen. He said that a terrible storm had broken towards the evening. So the sky played a part: it was the thunder and lightning that silenced the cannons. The Austrians had to retreat, utterly drenched. The two sides had been shooting at each other since six in the morning. It was a terrifying night, because the soldiers didn't know who had won; in the dark, every sound seemed to signal a new phase of battle.

Not once during this long narrative did Julien's eyes stray from his brother. Maybe he wasn't even listening, happy simply to be able to sit in front of him. I'll never forget that evening, in this empty, out-of-the-way café; while Louis was marching us across the blood-soaked fields of Solferino, we could hear the buzz of Paris out on the lash. When his brother had finished, Julien said quietly, 'So what? You're back. Who cares about anything else!'

In 1870, eleven years later, we were grown-ups. Louis was a captain. Julien, after dabbling in this and that, had slipped into the work-shy yet ever-so-busy lifestyle of the sort led by well-off Parisians who loiter at literary parties and first hangings without ever picking up a pen or a paintbrush. He'd published one decent collection of poems, but that was it – nothing more. I saw him now and again; he talked about his brother, posted to some garrison town out in the sticks.

The news that we would be at war with Germany was greeted with great enthusiasm. Talk all you like about how Napoleon III plunged France into conflict out of self-interest; you have to admit that the entire nation answered his call.[8] I'm only saying what I saw happening around me. There was a lot of hot-headed bluster about taking back our rightful border at the Rhine, and about getting revenge for Waterloo, which was a millstone around all our necks.[9] If only the campaign had started with a victory, France would surely have celebrated this war, instead of cursing it. Of course, had there been no fighting, we would have been disappointed, especially after the stormy exchanges in the Corps Législatif.[10] Once war was certain, every heart beat faster. I'm not talking about the crowds that were chanting on the boulevards, or the people who, allegedly, were paid to drum up support; I'm talking about the decent, hard-working majority who straight away traced out on maps the progress of our troops all the way into Berlin. We were going to drive back the Prussians with our rifle butts! Our complete confidence in the victory was a legacy of the days when our troops conquered all Europe. No danger of such jingoism these days.

On the Boulevard des Capucines one evening I saw crowds of men coming out of work and yelling *À Berlin! À Berlin!* Someone tapped me on the shoulder. It was Julien. He was grim-faced. I laughed, berating him for not getting behind the cause.

'We'll be beaten,' he said, quietly.

I argued, but he shook his head, without giving a reason. He had a feeling, he said. I asked him about his brother, who was already at Metz, and Julien showed me a cheerful letter that he had received the day before. The war would be a relief, wrote Louis; life in the barracks was killing him. He vowed to come home a colonel, wearing a medal.

With this letter I tried to convince Julien that he was being pessimistic.

'We'll be beaten.'

Paris was anxious again. I recognised the city's expectant silence; I'd heard it in 1859, before the opening battles of the Italian campaign. But this time the silence seemed more fearful. Nobody seemed to doubt victory; and yet there were ominous, unsourced rumours. It was a surprise, people said, that our forces hadn't taken the initiative and brought the fight behind enemy lines from the start.

One afternoon some big news broke on the Stock Exchange: we had pulled off a comprehensive victory, bagging a good haul of cannons and capturing a whole division. Homes were being decked out with bunting, and passers-by were hugging in the streets, when we were forced to recognise that this story was made up. There had been no battle. Such victories seemed only natural to me – indeed, predestined – but this hoax chilled me to the bone. The nation fell for it, being too quick to celebrate, and we had to save our glee for another day. I suddenly felt very sad; an unparalleled disaster was looming over our all our heads.

I'll remember that fateful day forever. Again it was a Sunday, and plenty of people must have thought of that glorious Sunday when Magenta fell. It was early August. No more radiant June sunshine; the air was heavy, and storm clouds lowered over Paris. I had been staying at a small town in Normandy; coming back, the city's deathly feel took me by surprise. Summer Sundays can be miserable, with their deserted streets and shuttered shops. But on this particular Sunday there was an extraordinary sense of doom. Groups of three or four people were scattered around the boulevards talking quietly. At last, I heard the terrible news: we were crushed at Froeschwiller,[11] and they were flooding into France.

I have never seen such panic. The whole of Paris was struck dumb. We lost! How could it have happened? The defeat seemed unjust, monstrous. It dealt a blow to our sense of patriotism, but it also destroyed our capacity to trust. The scale of the disaster was beyond us, at that time; we still hoped that our soldiers would have revenge. Nonetheless, we were ruined. There was deep shame in the city's sorry silence.

It was an awful afternoon, and an awful evening. The triumphant party atmosphere was a thing of the past. No come-hither smiles from passing women; no strangers making friends. A despairing city was shrouded in blackest night. No fireworks in the street, and no lanterns at windows. Early the next morning I saw a regiment marching down the boulevard. People stopped to watch, looking sad, and the soldiers passed with their heads hung low, as if they were responsible for the defeat. Nobody applauded. I had watched the victory parade after the Italian campaign come marching through this very same spot, when the reception had been earth-shaking. Nothing saddened me more.

The terrible, nervous wait began. Every two or three hours I went to the door of the city hall on the Rue Drouot, in the 9th, where they put up the telegrams. There were always people waiting, sometimes as a many as a hundred odd. They weren't noisy; they talked in hushed tones, as though keeping vigil in a sickroom. The minute a clerk stuck a telegram on the notice board, we rushed to read it. But for a long time there was only bad news, and the panic deepened. Even today I can't walk down the Rue Drouot without thinking of those wretched times. There, on that pavement, the people of Paris had to suffer the most painful torture. We heard the gallop of German troops getting closer, hour by hour.

I saw Julien often. He didn't crow about having predicted the defeat. He seemed merely to think that what had happened made perfect sense. Many Parisians were still shrugging their shoulders at the idea that the city could come under siege.[12] A *siege*: was that even possible? Others sought to demonstrate, as if by mathematical proof, that there could be no blockade of Paris. With a prescience that struck me only later, Julien declared that we would be surrounded on the 20th of September. He was still the schoolboy who loathed physical exercise. This war business was interrupting his routine; he wasn't himself. Why in God's name did people need to kill each other? He raised his hands to the heavens in protest. Yet he read all the dispatches eagerly.

'Were it not for Louis,' he insisted, 'I'd be writing poems, waiting for all this to end.'

He got letters from Louis only very rarely. The news was terrible; the troops were losing heart. The day we heard about Borny,[13] I met Julien at the corner of the Rue Drouot. Paris had a glimmer of hope that day. There was talk of victory. But Julien seemed even more despondent than normal. He had read somewhere that his brother's regiment had, in performing heroically, suffered severe losses.

Three days later a mutual friend came to tell me the awful news. Julien had received a letter the day before, informing him that his brother was dead. A shell blast had killed him at Borny. I ran straight away to the poor boy's digs; I found no one. The next morning I was still in bed when a tall young man called, dressed as a *franc-tireur*.[14] It was Julien. At first I didn't recognise him. Then I hugged him tight, tears in my eyes. He didn't cry. He sat down for a moment, waving away my pity.

'You see,' he said, quietly, 'I wanted to say goodbye to you. Now that I'm on my own, I'll get bored just doing nothing… I found out that a company of *franc-tireurs* was setting off, so I put my name down yesterday… It'll keep me busy.'

'When do you go?'

'Couple of hours… Goodbye!'

He hugged me back. I didn't dare quiz him further. He left, and I thought of him always.

After the catastrophe at Sedan,[15] and some days after the siege of Paris, I got some news. Our boy, who was so pale, so girlish, fought like a wolf – so one of his comrades told me. He was a savage, lurking in the bushes, preferring knives to guns. He stayed on the lookout all night long, hunting men like game; if anyone crossed his path, he slit their throat. I couldn't speak. This couldn't be Julien. Had this timid poet really become a butcher?

Now Paris was cut off from the rest of the world. The siege started; it was thrilling and soporific by turns. I couldn't go out without thinking of winter nights back in Aix. The streets were deserted, with homes shuttered down early. You could hear cannons and gunfire in the distance, of course, but the sound seemed to lose its way in the mournful silence of this vast city. Some days, there'd be hope in the air: the people would rouse themselves and forget about the long queues at the baker's, about the rations, about the unlit stoves, about the shells that rained down on the left bank. Then some new disaster would leave everyone dazed, and the silence would begin again: the silence of a city on the verge of dying. Yet during this long siege I did glimpse corners of undisturbed happiness: people making do, not willing to sacrifice their everyday walk in the bright winter sunshine; lovers who smiled at one another in their suburban hideaway, deaf to the sound of shelling. You lived one day at a time. All our illusions were shattered. We waited for a miracle. Provincial garrisons might come to rescue us, or maybe there'd be a mass evacuation, or some other extraordinary measure that would be taken when the time was right.

One day I was at one of the outposts when a man was brought in after having been found in a ditch. I recognised Julien. He insisted on speaking to a general so that he could pass on intelligence. I stayed with him all night. He hadn't slept in a bed since September, refusing to delegate his cutthroat duties. He didn't reveal much, only shrugging his shoulders and saying that it was the same thing every time: he killed as many Prussians as he could, however he could, with his gun or with his knife. Overall, he said, it was a very dull life, and much less dangerous than you'd think. He had never been in any real danger, except once when the French accused him of spying and were about to shoot him.

The next day, he said he was going back, into the fields, into the woods. I begged him to stay in Paris. We were at my place; he was sitting down, he didn't seem to hear. Suddenly, he said:

'You're right. Enough… I killed my share.'

Two days later, he told me that he had just joined the cavalry. I was speechless. Hadn't he avenged his brother enough then? Or was he in the grip of some new-found patriotism? I smiled.

'I'm covering for Louis, so it's soldier or nothing for me. Ah… gunpowder! *Homeland*, you see, it's the ground where the ones you loved lie sleeping.'

NOTES

1. In 1783 Russia annexed the Crimea, a Ukrainian peninsula, from Turkey. When religious tension caused these two nations to fight the Crimean War (1853–6), France – fearing Russian expanionism, like its ally Britain – intervened on the side of the Turks. 'The Italian campaign' (1859) bolstered Sardinia in its war against Austria, rulers of the northern regions Lombardy and Venetia since 1815. 'The catastrophe of 1870' refers to the Franco-Prussian War (1870–1), which Emperor Napoleon III declared and lost.

2. In September 1855 Franco-British troops seized the Ukrainian port city, a key Russian naval base, after an eleven-month siege.

3. In 1830 Victor Hugo (1802–85) scored a controversial hit with the play *Hernani*, a courtly romance set in sixteenth-century Spain, which challenged the prevailing artistic fashion for seeking inspiration in Classical antiquity. *Hernani* helped to inaugurate a phase of literary Romanticism, of which Alfred de Musset (1810–57) was a central (if ambivalent) figure. Zola admired Hugo and Musset as a young man, but criticised them repeatedly in later life. 'Lettre à la Jeunesse' ('Letter to the Youth', 1880), for instance, argued that Hugo's poetic idealism was 'dangerous', 'leading young people into… lies' and 'vice'. Zola promoted his own earthy Naturalism as the remedy: it 'may be frightening', he conceded, 'but not corrupting'.

4. Saint-Cyr is a military academy in Brittany, founded in 1803.

5. The Franco-Sardinian alliance defeated the Austrians at this northern Italian town on 4th June 1859.

6. A newspaper, founded in 1789, regarded – at the point in time that Zola describes – as an official organ of Napoleon III.

7. On 24th June 1859, Franco-Sardinian forces fought Austrian troops for more than nine hours at this northern Italian town; both sides suffered heavy losses.

8. Napoleon III's declaration of war on Prussia came amid mounting domestic demands for democratic reform.

9. The Congress of Vienna (1814–5) redrew European borders in the wake of the ultimately disastrous Napoleonic Wars (1803–15) between France and its rival continental powers; an alliance of English and Prussian forces inflicted on Napoleon Bonaparte his final defeat at the Battle of Waterloo (18th June 1815).

10. The *Corps Législatif* is the chamber of elected representatives, where the prominent anti-Imperialist Adolphe Thiers (1797–1877) denounced plans to attack Prussia.

11. Prussian troops seized the Alsatian village of Froeschwiller on 6th August 1870.

12. The Prussians' nineteen-week siege of Paris began on 19th September 1870.

13. On 14th August 1870, the retreating French forces delayed their westward withdrawal to fight a bloody battle at Borny in Lorraine, east of Metz.

14. The decisive battle of the Franco-Prussian War was fought on 1st September 1870 at Sedan, a north-eastern town near the border with Belgium; Napoleon III surrendered with 17,000 men killed or wounded, and more captured. A Republic was declared on 4th September, while fighting continued for a further five months.

In Paris, a popular revolt at the circumstances of the defeat led to a two-month period of rule under 'the Commune', brutally repressed during the 'Bloody Week' of 21st–28th May 1871.

Emile Zola was born in April 1840 and grew up in Aix-en-Provence, where he befriended the artist Paul Cézanne. In 1858, Zola moved to Paris with his mother. Despite her hopes that he would become a lawyer, he in fact failed his baccalaureate, and went on to work for the publisher Hachette, and to write literary columns and art reviews. He lost his job at Hachette on publication of his autobiographical novel, La Confession de Claude (1865), before his earliest venture into naturalistic fiction, Thérèse Raquin (1867). His series of twenty volumes, Les Rougon-Macquart (1871–93) is a natural and social history of one family under the Second Empire in France, individual volumes exploring social ills and the influence of nature and nurture on human nature. L'Assommoir (1877) concerned drunkenness and the Parisian working classes, Nana (1880) addressed sexual exploitation, and Germinal (1885) considered labour conditions. Other novel sequences followed, always entailing vast amounts of research. Zola's later life as a writer was famously punctuated by his involvement in the Dreyfus affair, in which a Jewish army officer was falsely accused of selling military secrets to the Germans. In a newspaper letter entitled 'J'accuse' (1898), Zola challenged the establishment and invited his own trial for libel, the author later removing briefly to England to escape the subsequent prison sentence. Emile Zola died in 1902, apparently asphyxiated by carbon monoxide fumes when asleep. Naturalism declined after his death, but his depictions of 'Nature seen through a temperament' were an important influence on writers such as Theodore Dreiser and August Strindberg.

HESPERUS PRESS

Hesperus Press is committed to bringing near what is far – far both in space and time. Works written by the greatest authors, and unjustly neglected or simply little known in the English-speaking world, are made accessible through new translations and a completely fresh editorial approach. Through these classic works, the reader is introduced to the greatest writers from all times and all cultures.

For more information on Hesperus Press, please visit our website: **www.hesperuspress.com**

SELECTED TITLES FROM HESPERUS PRESS

Author	Title	Foreword writer
Pietro Aretino	*The School of Whoredom*	Paul Bailey
Pietro Aretino	*The Secret Life of Nuns*	
Jane Austen	*Lesley Castle*	Zoë Heller
Jane Austen	*Love and Friendship*	Fay Weldon
Honoré de Balzac	*Colonel Chabert*	A.N. Wilson
Charles Baudelaire	*On Wine and Hashish*	Margaret Drabble
Giovanni Boccaccio	*Life of Dante*	A.N. Wilson
Charlotte Brontë	*The Spell*	
Emily Brontë	*Poems of Solitude*	Helen Dunmore
Mikhail Bulgakov	*Fatal Eggs*	Doris Lessing
Mikhail Bulgakov	*The Heart of a Dog*	A.S. Byatt
Giacomo Casanova	*The Duel*	Tim Parks
Miguel de Cervantes	*The Dialogue of the Dogs*	Ben Okri
Geoffrey Chaucer	*The Parliament of Birds*	
Anton Chekhov	*The Story of a Nobody*	Louis de Bernières
Anton Chekhov	*Three Years*	William Fiennes
Wilkie Collins	*The Frozen Deep*	
Joseph Conrad	*Heart of Darkness*	A.N. Wilson
Joseph Conrad	*The Return*	Colm Tóibín
Gabriele D'Annunzio	*The Book of the Virgins*	Tim Parks
Dante Alighieri	*The Divine Comedy: Inferno*	
Dante Alighieri	*New Life*	Louis de Bernières
Daniel Defoe	*The King of Pirates*	Peter Ackroyd
Marquis de Sade	*Incest*	Janet Street-Porter
Charles Dickens	*The Haunted House*	Peter Ackroyd
Charles Dickens	*A House to Let*	
Fyodor Dostoevsky	*The Double*	Jeremy Dyson
Fyodor Dostoevsky	*Poor People*	Charlotte Hobson
Alexandre Dumas	*One Thousand and One Ghosts*